Happy Easter Jill

Love

Cameron + Kristine

The Fuzzy
Duckling

THE FUZZY
DUCKLING

BY JANE WERNER
PICTURES BY ALICE AND MARTIN PROVENSEN

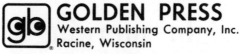

GOLDEN PRESS
Western Publishing Company, Inc.
Racine, Wisconsin

Copyright 1949 by Western Publishing Company, Inc.
All rights reserved. Produced in U.S.A.

0-307-10841-4
Sixth Printing, 1976

Early one bright morning
a small fuzzy duckling went for a walk.

He walked through the sunshine.
He walked through the shade.

In the long striped shadows
that the cattails made
he met two frisky colts.

"Hello," said the duckling.
"Will you come for a walk with me?"
But the two frisky colts would not.

So on went the little duckling,
on over the hill.
There he found three spotted calves,
all resting in the shade.
"Hello," said the duckling.

"Will you come for a walk with me?"
But the sleepy calves would not.
So on went the duckling.

He met four noisy turkeys

and five white geese

and six lively lambs
with thick soft fleece.

But no one would come for a walk
with the fuzzy duckling.
So on he went, all by his lone.

He met seven playful puppies

and eight hungry pigs.
"Won't you come for a walk with me?"
asked the fuzzy duckling.
"You had better walk straight home,"
said the pigs.

"Don't you know it's supper time?"
"Oh," said the duckling. "Thank you."
And he turned around to start for home.
But which way was home?

Poor little duckling.
He walked this way and that,
but he could not find the right path.

Just as he began to feel quite unhappy,
he heard a sound in the rushes near by...
and out waddled nine fuzzy ducklings
with their big mother duck.

"At last," said the mother duck.
"There is our lost baby duckling."

"Get in line," called the other ducklings.
"We're going home for supper."

So the lost little duckling joined the line,
and away went the ten little ducklings,
home for supper.

"This is the best way to go for a walk,"
said that happy little, fuzzy little duck.